# A Battleaxe and a Metal Arm 12:

# *A Promise of Winter*

Samuel Fleming

Cover Art by David Leahey

ISBN-13: 978-1-954679-33-7 (paperback)
ISBN-13: 978-1-954679-32-0 (ebook)

Thank you to my Beta Readers

and to my First Reader,

Mel.

iv

# Contents

"Death hath made us weary."
—unknown

# Previously...

After narrowly escaping the Idnauthi ship, the heroes and the surviving Terrans wandered the attic of the castle. Helesys kindled her warding light to lead them and keep the denizens of the attic at bay—the faceless Terrans. They had already witnessed an attack by the creatures first-hand, and the featureless visage of Sigun, their Idnauthi tormentor, still lingered at the edge of the light. They were weary, and Helesys was afraid to sleep, lest the light go out, but the voice of her wand reassured her, and soon they found a passage down from the attic.

They stepped onto a catwalk that spanned a misty green void. The faceless creatures from the attic could not follow them into the light. In the silence, Helesys and the elven survivors spoke, and she finally learned several answers: She had lived as both royalty in the one elven city, Novissimé, and been a soldier in the Eternal War.

Soon they passed grisly tubes carrying the separated remains of a Terran—blood, organs, bones, and clothes. The catwalk turned straight down and the Terrans continued their journey, defying gravity as they walked toward the bottom of the realm. They passed strange fish as they journeyed deeper, their shapes and sizes as limitless as the dungeon itself.

The heroes and survivors passed unnoticed by the strange fish, until they came to the mermaids. The eerie creatures tried to convince the heroes to leap from the railings and swim, and when the group refused, the mermaids tried to pull them over the side. The walkway became a maelstrom of claws, blades, and blasts. Young Scarlett was pulled over and a mermaid swam away with her, but Shawn leapt over the side, plummeting into the depths after them. Helesys was forced to call on the Ring of Winter to drive the mermaids away. In the quiet aftermath, Shawn walked toward them from the mist, carrying the uninjured Scarlett.

Hours later, they reached the floor. They continued, surrounded by mist, until spinning white walls sprung up around them, enclosing them. From the mist came eerie visages of the heroes and the Terrans—mirrors of themselves. Helesys called on power and bested her mirror by beating it with icy impacts from the Gar of Shéslang and the Ring of Winter.

When her own battle was won, she turned and cast a blight spell upon the others; the spell causing the misty mirrors to falter just long enough for her allies to best them. Taunauk wrested the axe from his enemy's hands, cleaving through it. Shawn stabbed his mirror in the back, then the pair set to aiding the survivors. When all was over, the white walls disappeared, leaving them to continue.

They found a crater of ash and followed the guidance of Shawn's coin and Helesys's wand down the powdery slopes. Glass tubes rose out of the ground like sparse, twisted bramble—similar to the grisly tubing from the walkway above. The mist began to clear. They passed shimmering pools of silver and white, then horrid growths of blood and glass.

Along the way, Helesys and her wand spoke of magic-imbued items, how some were made for singular purpose, while others, like the wand, were made for more—for a special soldier and the Eternal War.

Soon the growths of blood and glass became a forest, the branches combining into archways, and growing into a city. Finally, the mist cleared completely, and the Terrans could see the bleeding city stretching out to a pink spire that reached up into the ends of the realm.

The visage of Mr. Mask appeared in the bloody muscle of a nearby tree, spoke to them and told them that they were not ready to leave. The true body of Mr. Mask came down from the crystalline spire—a terrible spider-like titan—and strode across the landscape and stood over them.

It called forth creatures from the trees: More visages—this time in the likeness of Helesys's mother and sister, and other beloved memories from her comrades. They spoke in shadowed truths, and were not felled as easily as the mirrors from before. Helesys's mother whispered love while her sister whispered of Helesys's failure. In the end, the weaver called Aradi a liar, and blasted a hole through her chest before turning her gauntlet on the other memories.

Then Helesys turned her power toward Mr. Mask and the blistered landscape. She reached out for the lost voices and buried souls, then bolstered them, expanding their power as she once had the Apothecary in the cannibal realm. The souls became a boiling sea, and a cacophony rose that pulled Mr. Mask beneath the waves.

As the realm collapsed, the heroes ran. Suddenly aware that the green lights of the mist had gone, and the faceless Terrans of the attic were storming the realm. By the time the heroes and survivors made it to the central spire and the seam, the faceless mass stood behind them, crowding the halls—only kept at bay by Helesys's warding light.

In the end, Helesys opened the seam to the frozen realm of the Godpeak, leaving the faceless Terrans to tear apart the realm of Mr. Mask.

The heroes woke in that familiar starting room, snow pouring in from down the hall. Then they threw snow, celebrating the fleeting peace.

~ ~ ~

# *Foreboding*

Taunauk said, "It looks like there is a village down the hill, and the Godpeak is in the distance."

The heroes and survivors walked from the familiar starting room and through the snow-covered hall, dodging snowballs from the young ones.

Soon they had passed through the hall, and out onto the snow-covered hillside and the howling wind. Some ways to the left, at the bottom of the slope, were the soft lights. Though it was impossible to see details through the snow, Helesys knew why Taunauk had assumed it was a village. The lights were still and constant, and every now and then, the wind would die down enough that Helesys could just make out buildings in the distance.

To the right, the snowy hills extended all the way to the foot of the Godpeak, and the deep blue mountain rose up into the swirling snow.

All eyes fell on the ominous mountain, and they were silent except for the wind.

Helesys had looked upon the monstrous landscapes of the castle—the dungeon: The infinite wall, the wode and the jungle, the endless sea, the cavern of Shéslang, One-Mind's realm of metal, and Mr. Mask's blistered city… None so far had dwarfed them like this mountain. Even staring at only the foot of it, the weaver felt humbled.

They had come to the realm for answers—Taunauk to commune with the spirits he carried, and both Helesys and Shawn came to find their memories. It was fitting that such a pivotal point in their journey should come only after scaling such a thing.

At the beginning of their journey, when they first woke, Helesys swore that she would do anything to find answers and anything to escape. With quiet resolve, she renewed those vows.

Whatever dangers waited on the Godpeak, they would not stand in Helesys's way.

~

They set toward the village first. Only Helesys, Taunauk, and Shawn were willing to make the journey up the Godpeak.

The weaver was glad for that, for it was a miracle that they'd been able to protect the survivors of the Idnauthi ship for so long. As much as Helesys would protect them, she was ready to leave them somewhere safe.

Helesys's wand kept the group warm, kindling their own innate fortitude or warmth. In spite of their meager clothing, they suffered the gales as if they were a cool spring breeze.

But splitting her magic in so many directions was tricky. As powerful as her wand was, even it had limits. Helesys chuckled at this—that concentrating on such a mundane task should trouble her wand so, when it could bring such potent, even catastrophic, power to bear at other times.

*We are made for different things*, the wand whispered to her. *You and I were made to be weapons, not fireplaces.*

Helesys replied, *Maybe in our next life we will be so lucky. To live as something quiet and mundane.*

*Perhaps for you. If I were just a mundane wand, I would not exist.*

Helesys smiled, then turned to her comrades.

She walked in toward the middle and the right of the group. Taunauk led, and Shawn followed close behind.

No one talked—the wind was far too loud to keep up a conversation. And Helesys found herself glancing back intermittently toward the rogue.

Shawn met her eyes twice when she did this, both times giving her an animated thumbs up.

Still, she worried about Shawn. Though he had his own powers, he seemed sensitive to cold. Despite magic warmth, she saw him rub his arms as if fighting off a chill.

Two other times she'd seen him succumb to cold—in Amadeus's vast greenhouse, the very same place where she'd gotten the Ring of Winter, then again, when she'd used the ring too close to him. She'd hoped that it was something to do with the artifact, but seeing Shawn against the mundane cold, she wasn't convinced.

She resolved to bring it up once they'd reached the village and, hopefully, found shelter.

~

Time and distance blurred together in the snow. Trudging through the thick snow was already wearing on the little ones, many of which found themselves on the back of an adult.

Helesys judged that they had walked some two miles, but the lights of the village still seemed faint.

Taunauk waved for Helesys. He was scanning the hillside with quiet intensity. White flakes clung to the stubble on his head and face, and caked the fur of his cloak. It made the weaver think of her own hair tucked down the back of her cloak—it was short and given length by illusion. No flakes would stick to her hair.

When she was near, he spoke just loud enough to be heard over the wind. "Something is wrong. Do you feel it?"

Helesys reached out with her gauntlet, now covered with a thin layer of frost. There was magic—a thin veil of it. Her wand didn't hum in danger, only in vague recognition.

She nodded to Taunauk. "It might be an illusion."

The Endroggen grumbled. "How is your magic holding?"

"It will hold." Reluctantly, she added, "I'm glad we don't have more with us."

Taunauk nodded, taking her meaning. He knew that her magic had limits, and she knew enough not to give breath to fate: The kindled warmth would hold, so long as she wasn't forced to split her magic more ways.

They walked only a few steps farther before her wand hummed with familiar warning. Helesys grit her teeth. "It's a trap!"

The hillside rumbled, and the warriors among them readied their weapons. Walls of snow rose up around them—encircling them.

Helesys felt her tenuous power, so focused on keeping them warm, and split the little left to bolster her strength and her arcane blast—then she compounded them with the frost-covered spear. The Gar of Shéslang answered, always ready for battle, and the weaver held the delicate balance and waited.

Shadows walked behind the mottled wall of snow and ice. Moments later, a person appeared at the top of the wall. They held a crystalline staff and peered down at them from behind a thick fur coat.

"It's been a long time since Terrans made it this far down the slope, with a weaver, no less." The woman's voice was firm and the staff glowed softly. "Tell us what you want."

Taunauk answered, "Shelter for most. Safe passage to the Godpeak for three of us."

The mage disappeared behind the wall again, and Helesys watched vague shapes through the ice. She imagined they were discussing what to do with their group. The moment dragged on, and Helesys's arm began to ache.

The mage finally came back to the top of the wall and called down, "You come ready for war. How do we know that we can trust you?"

Taunauk replied, "We have children with us. And you have our word."

There was the slightest nod from the fur-covered mage. "Relax your wand, weaver."

For a moment, Helesys did nothing, but her wand's warning had relaxed. In spite of that, Helesys had to force herself to relax.

Helesys stared at the woman and nodded reluctantly. She relaxed the power from the spear and from her wand-arm—holding only the kindled warmth for her comrades.

"I have let go of all that I can. The rest is warmth that sustains us."

The mage's crystal staff grew brighter, and Helesys felt that the woman was judging her power—seeing if Helesys told the truth about it. The mage stepped away from the edge, and moments later, the ground shuddered as the icy walls sunk back into the hill.

There were a half a dozen fur-clad figures surrounding them—hoods pulled tight over their faces. Three held staves, the others, swords. Beyond them, the lights of the village were much brighter than before. Either they had been teleported closer, or the illusion spell had concealed the true distance to the village.

The mage with the crystal staffed called over the wind, "Follow us, and do not stray." Then she led them into the snow-covered village.

~ ~ ~

# Respite

What at first had seemed a village composed of log cabins was actually an illusion. The lighted windows and wood sides were little more than snow banks.

In actuality, the dwellings were little more than giant mounds of snow. There might have been two dozen mounds in varying sizes; the smallest looked around twelve feet across, while two were nearly fifty feet long. There were no windows or doors to mark the dwellings. It wasn't until Helesys passed close to one that she saw a narrow short tunnel that dipped into the snow and under the wall of the dwelling.

Yellow lights hung in the air around the village. Helesys was reminded of the glowing blue faeries, except that these lights had no form—they were little more than balls of pure magic.

The mages and warriors ushered the group toward one of the two large mounds. One of the warriors pointed to the narrow tunnel, then climbed through, expecting the rest of them to do the same.

Taunauk insisted on going first, but had to take both Everfall and axe from his backslings to do so. He pushed both weapons through the narrow tunnel, then shimmied through. The whole of the Idnauthi survivors went next. Then Shawn.

Then Helesys crawled into the small tunnel. In spite of the magic warmth within her, she felt the temperature drop and was glad that she already saw the end of it. The magic spear was just short enough that she could maneuver it through without trouble. She quickly reached the other side and climbed out.

She stood in the icy cavern and was immediately taken aback. However long the room had appeared on the outside, it was twice as large on the inside. It must have been fifteen feet high and nearly a hundred long. The whole of it was dimly lit by the same floating balls of light. Second, she noticed the dwelling was much warmer than outside. The weaver could no longer see her breath, and the icy walls seemed to glisten with perspiration. She tentatively relaxed her kindled warmth and found the air cool and pleasant in contrast to the outside realm.

There was a narrow walkway through the center of the room, at the end of this lay wicker baskets of frilly green plants. To either side were raised platforms of ice, waist high to the weaver. These raised areas wrapped around the edge of the walls and joined in the center, and were covered in all manner of furs and ragged pillows. A half dozen Terrans lounged about the platform, some laying against wicker half-chairs—all turned to consider the newcomers, and silence filled the room.

Helesys found herself smiling at the people and the design of the structure. Heat rose, and so the sitting areas were no-ticeably warmer than the lower floor and the passage to the outside. It was science—magic without magic.

Soon, the other mages and warriors had climbed into the long dwelling and sifted toward the end. They pulled their hoods back to reveal an assortment of Terrans—humans, elves, and even an orc.

The mage with the crystalline staff was a thin elven woman with long dark hair and piercing blue eyes. "My name is Emilee, and you can stay here for the meantime. You will find our longhouse suitable." She gestured to the wicker baskets on the floor. "You may help yourselves to our stores—lichen and snowberries. We will bring you furs as well. Do not think it generous, for if you wish to stay here, then you will be expected to forage and earn your keep. It can be harsh here, but it is sustainable."

For a moment, the Idnauthi survivors looked to Helesys, Taunauk, and Shawn for an answer. But Helesys replied, "It is not our place to answer for you."

But laced within her words was an answer, one that both survivors and heroes already knew: There were few safe harbors in the realms, little chance that the survivors would find another place such as this. The heroes could not keep them safe forever. Nor would they stop in their pursuit to defeat the Wolf King and escape the dungeon.

The Idnauthi survivors looked between each other uneasily, no doubt already knowing their answer. After a moment, Scarlett's mom, Isabella, spoke up. "We agree."

~

The people had named the icy village, Lamoral, and they welcomed the heroes and the survivors with compassion and open arms. The longhouse became their temporary home, and they were encouraged to rest, to eat, and to share their stories.

A divide emerged in the longhouse. Toward the entrance, the Idnauthi survivors sat and ate with members of the village.

Their spirits lifted. Scarlett and the few other children even clung tight to wicker dolls. For a moment, Helesys did not recognize them—it was as if the toys had erased the hard journey.

At the back of the longhouse, the mage, Emilee, and a human warrior named Sozen, ate tentatively with Helesys, Taunauk, and Shawn. Occasionally, Helesys caught flashes of a smile on the young man's face as he glanced at the three adventurers. The group sat cross-legged on furs, sharing a bowl of lichen and berries between them, a pleasant mixture of salt and sweetness. Only Shawn laid down completely, picking at the berries and occasionally scrunching handfuls of the soft fur in his hands.

Emilee and Sozen reassured them that the survivors would be well cared for. The village survived on a mixture of foraging and magic. Lichen and snowberries were plentiful, if one knew where to dig. And there were roving herds, motley assortments of caribou, elk, and sveltdeer. That was where the village got their furs.

Lamoral was several hundred years old, giving shelter to four generations of villagers—all orphans or wanderers that happened upon the village. Much of it had been carved from the snow and ice by hand, only later being reinforced and enlarged with magic. Helesys pointed out the ingenious use of heat sinks and elevated sleeping areas, to which Sozen explained that his people made their home in such places in the Frozen Isles in the South. It was likely a people akin to his that originally made Lamoral—carving out their own safe haven in the frost.

Emilee explained that most do not make it past the illusory trap between the stone hallway and the village—that most did not make it even that far in the frost. It also kept predators away, those that followed the herds: Wolves, yetis, frozen ghouls, rays, fire-bellies, and giant owls.

When the moment lulled, Sozen asked them of their journey. A hint of excitement flashed across his eyes, one that he seemed to actively suppress.

Together, the heroes told of their journey through the realms. Helesys and Taunauk spoke in turns, while Shawn added witty interjections. Gradually, they told the Emilee and Sozen of the fantastic and horrifying realms they had visited, and of the myriad of beings that had helped them along the way.

Both Emilee and Sozen listened intently, but were both taken aback at mention of the heroes walking between realms. Emilee grew quiet, while Sozen grew wide eyed.

But it was when Taunauk mentioned bringing relics back after death and across realms that both exchanged a concerned look.

"They should speak with O'Ten," Sozen said quietly.

"O'Ten does not take visitors."

"She would speak with *them*." A silence passed between them.

Helesys had been about to ask, but Shawn was quicker. "Who is O'Ten?"

Emilee replied, "O'Ten was one of the original founders of Lamoral. Life was so peaceful here that she lived until he died of old age. Then like all others, she was reborn and sent to wander again… She is the only one that has ever found their way back here. She was already old in her second life here when I came. O'Ten rarely speaks anymore… But Sozen is right. She just might speak with you.

"I will confer with the elders and if they are in agreement, I will take you to meet her."

~

Emilee and Sozen left the heroes at the end of the long-house. Silence hung between Helesys, Taunauk, and Shawn, and they merely watched the Idnauthi survivors and the villagers sharing food and stories.

Helesys mind drifted back to scant memories of her life before, mostly of her mother and her sister. Now, those bittersweet images were clouded by their journey through the previous realm of the twisted visage Mr. Mask had conjured against her—of having to fight her mother and her sister.

It was a turmoil of emotions that the weaver was only now starting to process.

In the moment, Helesys had assumed that the apparitions were lying to them... Or, at least, that her sister, Aradi, was lying.

*You always lie*, Helesys had said back to her sister. She felt that much to be true. The more she dwelled on her sister, the more Helesys felt that the Aradi couldn't be trusted—that she had betrayed her somehow. Maybe more than once.

But... had the visages been lying? Her mother's words: Not knowing why Helesys left and pleading for her to return. And then her sister's words: *Fail at another mission*, that Helesys had changed her mind, and finally—*you can't even die right*.

"I think my sister tried to kill me," Helesys whispered, just loud enough for Taunauk and Shawn to hear.

Taunauk turned to her, and Shawn propped himself up on his elbow.

Shawn said, "That's, uh, something."

Helesys turned back to her comrades, leaving the jovial survivors and villagers to their own devices. Then the weaver explained what the visages of her mother and her sister said to her. After she finished, Helesys added, "I don't think Mr. Mask's creations lied to us. I think they spoke the truth... Or perhaps a twisted version of it."

Taunauk and Shawn exchanged solemn glances, both reluctant to speak.

The Endroggen sighed. "The thing appeared as my father. It said... It said that all my life I have been alone. And that it would always be that way."

Shawn meekly added, "That's even worse, but also not true. You have us."

Taunauk flashed a meager smile. "It is as Helesys said: I feel it to be the truth."

"You lived in a tribe, didn't you?" Helesys asked. "How could you live there and be alone?"

Taunauk shook his head quickly—not that he didn't know, or that he didn't want to answer. That it pained him to answer.

"My father is dead," he whispered. His body grew very still, as if he could not bear to move. "I am sure of it."

"What about the spirits with you?" she asked, watching him carefully.

"They are silent."

When Taunauk didn't continue, Shawn sat all the way up and held his knees tight. "I guess the bastard was prying into our memories, 'cause I saw my boy. Well, he's Galli. He's not my boy, not really. I saw a memory where Galli and his grandfather, Eugen, had taken me in. I worked beside the old man in the factory. I don't know for how long..." Shawn trailed off, shaking his head.

"What did he say?" Helesys asked.

"Oh, just that he missed me. He doesn't know why I left. Neither of them did. That he and his grandfather would get along without me… They survived before and they'll keep going." Shawn shook his head again, face wrinkled in sadness. "The little scamp. You know, I was hoping one of you guys had a happy memory."

Taunauk snorted. "In this place?"

At that, the three of them chuckled. It was a fleeting thing—not even happiness—absurdity—and it was gone as quick as a spark.

Helesys said quietly, "We'll find answers on the Godpeak. We must stay hopeful."

Shawn sniffled and wiped his nose on his sleeve. "Maybe this O'Ten guy will have more to say about it. Gods know there's probably some horrible shit up there standing in our way, right?"

Taunauk groaned, and Helesys hung her head.

"I know, I know," Shawn said. "Don't breathe on fate."

Helesys and Taunauk cracked smiles at the rogue's misquote. Shawn followed.

A moment later, Emilee entered the longhouse and walked to them.

"You look in good spirits," she said. "The elders agree. You should speak with O'Ten."

~

Emilee gave Shawn a thick fur cloak for the rogue to wear, and the three followed Emilee out of the dwelling, past the weary and the sleeping. The few Idnauthi survivors that were awake watched them leave.

They crawled back out into the snow and the biting wind. They pulled their cloaks taut and followed her across the village, past the snow-hidden dwellings, to a small mound at the outskirts of the village.

She stopped in front of the dwelling. "It is a small thing on the inside, but O'Ten will make it big enough for you."

Helesys asked, "You're not coming?"

Emilee shook her head. "Her words will be for you and you alone. When you're done, come back to the longhouse."

Shawn interjected, "If it's all the same to you. I'm going in first."

The rogue crouched down and disappeared into the passage. Helesys bid Emilee goodbye and followed behind, crawling through the short passage and into the dwelling.

Helesys climbed through and tentatively stood, something that surprised her. Just like the other dwelling, O'Ten's dwelling was bigger on the inside—dome-shaped and seemed to be growing. She watched the ceiling and the walls around her expand, if it could be described in such a way. It almost seemed as if the walls were a shroud that was merely *pushed back*. The room grew, several more floating candles flickering into existence, until the circular dwelling was some ten feet wide and just as tall.

Across from Helesys, sat a woman with deep set wrinkles, brilliant white hair, and an expression of calm on her face. O'Ten was covered in a mound of heavy furs, with a single arm reaching out. She pushed outward lazily with that arm, the dwelling expanding with her motion.

A moment later, she slipped her arm back beneath the pile of furs, and bid them to sit, her voice both warm and worn. The earthy smell of lichen and a sweet spice lingered in the air—one that Helesys did not know.

O'Ten looked at each of them in turn, her eyes bright and unblinking as she did. The three of them waited for her to speak.

Even with the furs on the ground, the small dwelling was noticeably colder than the longhouse had been. And even with his new fur cloak, Shawn suppressed a shiver. Without thinking, Helesys kindled the warmth inside them again, and the rogue breathed a sigh of relief.

"Thanks for that," Shawn whispered.

Finally, O'Ten said, "Emilee tells me that you have wandered far, and that you can bring treasures back with you after death." She waited until Helesys nodded before continuing. "Show me what you've won."

Helesys laid the Gar of Shéslang and the jade lemur totem in front of her, and held up the Ring of Winter for the old mage to see. Taunauk laid Everfall across his lap. Shawn laid two daggers in front of him: The first had a blade of dark iron and the handle was an opaque swirl of white and gray mist. The second was bright silver, with nine gems in the handle—three of which glowed the deep red color of blood.

O'Ten smiled softly. "There have been stories that permeate the realms of warriors and mages that rebel against the inexorable death. Until now, I thought them only stories; I trust you. I never thought I would see the likes of you—the *Chosen*."

"What stories have you heard?" the weaver asked.

"Only a few. Every so often, extraordinary individuals are chosen from among the rest. They're given a single ability—a simple difference from the others trapped here: They are able to bring treasures back with them after death. If they are driven, they can amass immense power, the likes of which others can only dream.

"The Chosen seek escape. And the death of the Wolf King is the only way."

Helesys glanced at the others and saw them nodding in agreement. "We have heard the same stories. The god serpent Shéslang told us that it had met other Chosen, and it lamented seeing us because that meant that the other Chosen had failed."

"The Wolf King lives," Shawn added, still clutching his cloak tightly. "We had a run in with him, or… something like that. Helesys saw him."

O'Ten nodded slowly. "I've long wondered what happened to the Chosen if they failed. One wonders where the tales of triumph are."

Again, Helesys looked to her comrades, for they had met so few they could talk to about such things. The weaver told O'Ten about the Voice on the beach, who claimed to be helping them, who claimed to give them the power to bring things back.

Helesys watched the old woman's expression carefully as she recanted the tale, but O'Ten gave no expression other than an intermittent nod.

When Helesys was done, O'Ten sighed deeply. "I've never heard mention of where the gift comes from, but then I've never spoken to the Chosen either. Have you heard from the voice again?"

"No," Helesys replied. "The Voice on the beach told us to seek Zhug and the Machine of Antrikaumora. In our travels, the mechanical god, One-Mind, helped us to traverse the seams between realms, and told us to seek answers on the Godpeak."

O'Ten chuckled at that. "So it would seem."

Shawn asked, "Have you ever gone up there?'

O'Ten shook her head. "Not for lack of trying, mind you. The sides of the mountain are beyond perilous, but some have made the ascent by taking the passages inside—some far less than you three. You will find answers."

Taunauk said, "We seek answers about our past lives, and memories come back in trickles. You have lived long. Do you remember your life before?"

The old mage smiled and her gaze fell somewhere between them, somewhere past the ice that surrounded them. "I remember some."

Shawn asked, "But how can that be?"

"With each passing year, more memories came back to me. But I was trapped here, and each year, I had more and more memories from my journey through the realms… How many memories can one truly hold? Not many, I think. And so, even as I remembered more, they were lost just as easily to the unstoppable march of time.

"I remember a saying from my people, from my life before. It says that inside each Terran, there are two people: The person they were, and the one they are becoming."

Taunauk replied, "One-Mind told us a similar philosophy. Others said that being trapped here was a gift… I feel beholden to a past that I cannot remember."

O'Ten said, "Then you three better not dally. The longer you stay here, the further you are from the past."

Helesys looked to her comrade and saw Taunauk hanging his head.

~

Helesys, Taunauk, and Shawn agreed to spend the night in the longhouse and set out for the Godpeak in the morning.

That evening, the heroes found respite with the villagers and the Idnauthi survivors. They shared lichen and berries, and the mages showed Helesys how to use magic to stretch her stores even further.

"The spell is *Baccanova*," Emilee told her. "A third of your normal rations will sate you."

The Terrans finished eating, and shared stories and songs, some from lives before, others from their time wandering the realms. Twice, villagers sung of O'Ten, while the old mage sat quietly and listened with the faintest hint of a smile. Scarlett and the other survivor children played games with the younger villagers. They played strange games, trading wicker sticks with one another, and others like charades that Helesys barely recalled from her life before.

It was then that Helesys noticed that there were few young children among the Lamoral. She recalled Emilee's words that they hadn't had visitors in years, and the words rang true now. The Idnauthi survivors brought with them the last children to come in several years. A village replenishes itself with the young, and Helesys hoped that Lamoral would last longer still.

The weaver watched Scarlett and the others play without a care, and she smiled often. Taunauk and Shawn were in similar spirits—Helesys couldn't recall ever seeing a smile so large on Taunauk's face, though Shawn's were as wicked and wild as ever.

As the evening winded down, and the villagers left the new arrivals to sleep, Helesys laid on the thick furs and thought that they were lucky to have known peace in such a frigid place. If only for an evening.

~

The next morning was one of the hardest that Helesys could remember—not because she was tired, but because she was content, and she could remember so few mornings like it. She stared up the icy roof of the longhouse, ran her elven and metal fingers through the fur beneath her back, and breathed deep.

There was a part of her that longed for such simple comforts. And there was the rest of her, the soldier, the weaver, the prisoner, that knew such things were lies. Her sister's face flashed across her mind—liar.

She heard the quiet voice of her wand, *Soon you'll have answers.*

*Not soon enough*, Helesys replied. Beside her, she heard Shawn grumbling.

"But it's so early," the rogue whimpered.

The weaver grumbled and sat up. Taunauk was already awake and putting on his leather armor, strapping his vest and leg grieves. Meanwhile, Shawn was still laying down and wiping his eyes.

Soon, the three of them were up, armored, and grabbing the last of their supplies.

Helesys turned to leave and found little Scarlett sitting up and staring at her, motionless.

"Will you ever come back?" Scarlett whispered.

Helesys walked to her and knelt. As the girl was sitting up on the sleeping platform, it brought them eye to eye with one another.

Scarlett stared. And in that moment, Helesys would've preferred the girl do anything else—yell or cry, or turn away from her. No, Scarlett just stared, waiting for an answer. A girl who had nearly been a slave—nearly died a lingering death—who was still a prisoner, and who might yet find some semblance of peace.

"No," Helesys finally said. She would not lie to the girl. "Even if we fail, I doubt we will see each other again."

Scarlett just stared back, and it felt as if the two of them were caught in a battle of wills.

Taunauk knelt beside her, and said to Scarlett, "It's okay to be sad."

The girl looked down at a spot of fur before turning back to them. "Are you sad?"

Taunauk replied, "Yes."

"You don't look like it."

"I got used to hiding it, but you don't need to do that. You are not an Endroggen."

Scarlett hung her head and quiet tears came. She reached out for the heroes. Helesys embraced her, and then Taunauk embraced her, each of their faces mirroring the girl's.

Helesys turned to see Shawn standing stoically. Frozen.

Scarlett whispered, "Can I have a hug, Mr. Shawn?"

"Oh gods," the rogue said. He stooped down and embraced her, his shoulders spasming with stifled sobs. "Be good now. Take care of your ma. *Listen* to her. All that stuff."

The night before, Emilee had set aside bundles of food for them to take with them on their journey. The three grabbed these, and then they left the longhouse and the village.

And Helesys could not help but think of the powerful entrance they had made into the survivor's lives, and the quiet with which they stole away that morning.

There were things that came easily to the weaver, surrendering to her soldier's training, deciphering spells and incantations, dividing her wand's power, even standing up to gods of the realm. Yet, it was harder to leave behind these Terrans that she had known for only a short time, and to entrust them to a village that she had known for even less.

~ ~ ~

# *The Hills*

The heroes pulled their cloaks and furs taut and trudged through the thick snow of the realm.

Helesys kindled warmth for the three of them, but Taunauk told her that he didn't need it.

"Save your magic," the Endroggen said, frost clinging to the stubble on his face. "Rage will sustain me."

Shawn interjected, "I, for one, welcome it. This place is absolutely miserable."

Helesys smirked, but ignored the rogue. "Is your rage for Scarlett?'

Taunauk grunted in affirmation. "For her, and for all the others we've left behind."

The barbarian's words fell upon the snow, and for a time they walked in silence. The wind grew to overshadow their crunching steps. Though Helesys watched the hills for signs of danger, she began to glance occasionally at her comrades to be certain they were still there—that she wasn't walking alone in the desolate white.

"Your rage," Helesys said over the wind, "you once called it blood magic. Has anyone other than an Endroggen learned it?"

Taunauk stopped in the snow and narrowed his eyes at her. The wind roared behind him.

"I could go for some rage right about now," Shawn said. "Especially if it would keep me warmer."

Without thinking, Helesys kindled her warmth more, and the rogue heaved a sigh of relief.

Finally, Taunauk answered. "I also said that it was a magic passed down through generations of my people. I have never known another to wield Endroggen rage."

He turned and continued walking, and the others followed.

Shawn said, "You guys keep talking about that jade lemur. That sure would be swell right now, wouldn't it?"

Helesys's eyes widened and she reached for the statuette in her pocket, but her enthusiasm immediately wavered.

The quiet voice of her wand whispered clearly what she already knew. *It will not work. It's far too cold for the thing.*

*But will it take the weight of the three of us?* Helesys asked.

*I think so.*

Helesys said over the wind, "Sorry, Shawn. It's too cold for the lemur."

Shawn grumbled. "You know, I'm starting to think you like walking."

~

The heroes walked over the rolling hills, and the Godpeak grew in the distance, a wall of white. Hours dragged on, all the while Helesys kindled warmth for her and Shawn. Taunauk asked for nothing.

Shapes appeared on the hills. Three vaguely upright, Terran forms. On their heads rose great sets of antlers, sprawling with intricacy, nearly as tall as the creatures were.

"Behind us," Shawn muttered.

The three heroes whipped around, weapons drawn and power kindled, to see one of the creatures standing before them, nearly close enough to touch.

Its skin was snow-white, and without blemish or line of muscle—giving it a nearly formless appearance save for Terran outline and proportions. It towered above them, and Helesys craned her head to see its face. Its face too, was eerie white with the faintest lines of lips and nose. Its eyes seemed little more than globes of ice, and Helesys could not tell if the creature looked at her or if it was staring somewhere across the hills.

Its two massive antlers were a woven bramble of ice, at first appearing to be nothing more than chaos. Thin strands of red and black hung throughout the points, as if a pile of thread had been spilled over them. But as Helesys stared, she noticed a symmetry amidst the chaos: The antlers had grown in interlocking circles akin to runes, though nothing that she recognized.

As close and as strange as the icy figure was, there was no warning from Helesys's wand. Whatever it wanted, it did not seem to be dangerous.

At the edges of her vision, four similar creatures towered silently over the hills.

"Is it one of those elk that Emilee told us about?" Shawn asked.

"No," Taunauk replied uneasily.

Helesys reached out with her wand, searching for words, and found… something. Her voice became ethereal, something akin to melting snow and biting wind.

"*We are going to the mountain,*" she said. "*We mean you no harm.*"

Slowly, the creature craned its neck and stared right at her with its white eyes. Its antlers cast a shadow over her.

"*We mean you no harm,*" it said in the same delicate voice. "*We merely watch.*"

"*Who are you?*"

"*Nothing of importance. Observers that time has forgot, and that have forgotten.*"

"Everything okay?" Shawn asked timidly. "You're doing that weird voice-thing again."

"Everything's fine," Helesys replied in a voice momentarily her own before turning back to the creature. "*We are going to the mountain. Can you show us where the inner passages are?*"

It looked toward the mountain with a slow and weary movement, and was silent.

Finally, it said, "*We do not remember—danger comes.*"

Abruptly, the creature fell backward like a tree being struck down. Helesys reached out instinctively for it, but as she touched the creature's hand, it turned to snow. The creature landed backward on the snowbank and collapsed into powdery white. In moments, the wind erased the outline of its passing.

"What did you say?" Shawn asked.

"It said danger was coming," Helesys answered. She turned in time to see the other creatures fall backward in the snow and vanish.

As Helesys stared at the hill where the creatures had been, a wave formed in the snow and stretched across the hill. For a moment, it looked like the entire hill was moving. As the wave rolled downward, Helesys could see faint swooping lines joining in the center to form a tail, like the silhouette of a giant bird beneath the snowbank.

Her comrades had already followed her gaze.

Taunauk said, "We should run to the Godpeak."

Shawn replied, "We can't outrun that thing!"

It was on them before Helesys could reply. Instead, she bolstered her strength and turned what else she could to her arcane blast.

The heroes leapt from the wave and over it. A writhing maw erupted from the snow, big enough to swallow a Terran whole and filled with jagged teeth. A flat body followed, dark leathery wings billowed from the snow.

Helesys soared over the creature, and saw the wavering body and spined tail as thick as an oak tree as the giant manta ray dove beneath the snow.

The three landed apart on the snowy hill, and Taunauk motioned for them to stay where they were: Helesys in the middle, Taunauk to her right, and Shawn to her left. They waited and watched as the snowy wave turned and came back toward them—directly toward them.

Taunauk grunted in frustration.

"What did you think would happen?" Shawn called.

"That if we didn't move, it wouldn't find us. Get ready!"

The ray barreled toward them like a tidal wave of snow. Even standing apart, the creature's wingspan easily stretched past them.

Helesys turned her gauntlet toward it and let power fly. Purple blasts soared over the snow and smashed into the wave. Snow and steam were sent into the air, but still the creature came. Only briefly did the gnashing teeth of the ray break the surface of the snow, and she could not hit it.

And as she fired, she watched the center of the wave turn, ever so slightly, toward her.

The wave was upon them and again Helesys leapt over the open mouth of the giant ray. This time, the creature lingered beneath her as it jumped high in anticipation of her jump. Its teeth passed a mere foot beneath her and it seemed to linger in the air, its great wings rippling in the chill wind. The creature crashed into the snow and Helesys landed behind the ray's flank. She ducked just as its whip-like tail to pass close over-head.

Shawn landed some yards away, unperturbed. Then, the weaver heard the roar of Taunauk. The barbarian leapt to the back of the ray before it disappeared beneath the snow, crashing down on it with a swing of his battleaxe.

Instead of slashing flesh, a sharp crack echoed over the hill, as if the blade had struck stone. The last thing Helesys saw was the axe embedded in the beast's back and Taunauk holding fast as the pair of them disappeared beneath the snow.

For a moment, there was no trace of the ray.

"Oh sh—"

Shawn's curse was cut short by snow erupting from the hill—the violent return of the beast. Taunauk roared. He was covered in snow drift, only the vaguest Terran outline of him discernable, and clung to the axe that was still stuck in the ray's back.

The ray thrashed and billowed like a giant sheet caught in a storm, but she couldn't hear the creature over the cry of the Endroggen.

Helesys reached out with her wand-arm, kindling power and magnifying it with the Gar of Shéslang.

*"Restu sonmova, planescis."*

The ray had reared back, nearly standing vertical in its desperation, like the sail of a warship. And with her words, it ceased struggling, and fell like a broken tower to the hill below. The impact shook the bank, but the creature did not move.

Helesys and Shawn ran up the hill and to the monster and the barbarian.

All the while, Helesys felt the mind of the giant ray. In her mindspace, it felt as if she were back in the strange walkways of the laboratory, walking beside the ray as it swam in the ether. She was dwarfed by the creature, yet it was the one that cowered—as if it was held in the grasp of some far larger predator.

She felt a pang of pity for the beast. As she ran, she muttered, "You left me no choice."

They came upon the scene. Taunauk stood tall for a moment, brushed the thick covering of snow from his front, then turned back to pulling his axe free.

"What's the matter? Don't have enough muscles?" Shawn called up.

Taunauk grumbled, still struggling. "Its flank is scaly and hard as stone."

"Need a hand?" the rogue asked.

"No."

Shawn looked from the ray to the mountain in the distance. "It's a shame we can't just ride it, you know? Instead of walking. *That* would be nice."

It was a ridiculous idea—Helesys nearly told Shawn just that. And yet… She had seen mages command creatures before. She'd watched in horror as the Wolf King had possessed the wizard, Amadeus, in his own sanctum, and made him move and cast spells. She'd seen the Idnauthi, Sigun, control other Terrans with his thoughts, and seen the insect queen do the same. Helesys thought back to the moments when Shawn had an Idnauthi slug in his head… Had she merely threatened the slug to get it to leave his head, or had she commanded it?

Helesys walked up to the creature, then climbed on its back. Taunauk paused and turned to her, still gripping the axe.

Shawn appeared beside her a moment later. "You can't actually do that, right? Right?"

Helesys ignored him and turned back to her mindspace, to the immobilized ray. It was doubtful that she could communicate more than simple things to the beast, but Helesys bid her wand to translate.

Instead of speaking, Helesys pictured the foot of the Godpeak and the beast gliding over the top of the snow toward it.

In her mindspace, the ray's wings fluttered in agitation—in refusal.

Helesys channeled more power, and again pictured what she wanted the beast to do. In the mindspace, Helesys grew large, until she towered over the ray.

And in the snow, the ray stirred, its great wings fluttering. It turned toward the Godpeak, the heroes catching their balance as it did.

Then it lurched forward, gliding across the tops of the hills. The three heroes rode the giant ray toward the foot of the Godpeak with a mix of concentration, stoicism, and wide-eyed joy.

~

Soon, the heroes were tearing across the snowy hills on the back of the giant ray. The rushing wind became a roar, and Helesys had to hide her face beneath the neck of her cloak and shunt even more power to her kindled warmth for her and Shawn.

Shawn stood to her right. He too pulled his cloak taut around him. Occasional shivers racked his body, and sucked the humor from his breath, but the rogue stayed on his feet. Taunauk stood stoically to her left, his own cloak trailing in the wind, still clutching the hilt of his axe while the blade lay embedded in the ray's back.

But more than the wind, Helesys felt growing nausea. Each spell had a different recoil, like that of a cannon or a punch colliding with flesh. She would feel pain, heat, or soreness in her metal arm or in her muscles. Other times the recoil was felt psychically.

Initially, Helesys had been confused by the sensation of guiding the ray across the snow. At first, a small part of her reveled in the display of power. She was no simple spellweaver, she was wielding a power displayed by masters of the realms. She'd pushed the ray faster and faster across the hills until the frigid air scalded her eyes and she watched the landscape through squints.

The beast's distress grew, and it quickly grew exhausted at the pace. This caused Helesys's stomach to turn.

She'd thought the mental recoil of driving the ray close to that of the blight spell, but it was much more subtle. Helesys could not command the ray without feeling what it felt—fatigue and primal fear. She felt pity for the creature, and then shame at what she was doing, at the needless antagonizing, like she was bullying a child or some defenseless creature.

She had to steady her breathing to suffer the last minutes to the Godpeak.

The ray traversed the hills and stopped at the foot of the mountain, mere feet from the stone. Helesys immediately leapt from its back, down to the snow, and wretched. Green bile melted into the white.

Soon after, she heard another crack, and the crunch of snow as her comrades leapt from its back. She turned back for a moment and saw the pair looking at her with concern—Taunauk with axe in hand.

Helesys tried to wave them away before she wretched again. She abruptly let go of her hold on the beast. The giant ray thrashed for a moment, hurling snow into the air, before diving under the white and traveling away from them.

"You, uh… You okay?" Shawn asked. Helesys nodded. The rogue added, "Because you don't look it."

Mercifully, the nausea was already passing. She focused on the kindled warmth inside her, and wiped her mouth and nose. She turned to face her comrades beneath the shadow of the Godpeak.

"I'm fine, now," she replied.

Taunauk eyed her. His eyes were narrowed and thick flakes of white clung to his face. "We each have our skills, but perhaps that isn't one of yours."

"I was curious," she replied. "Don't worry, I don't plan on doing that again."

Taunauk nodded, wearily. Then he turned and began to walk away. "We should look for the cavern entrance."

Meanwhile, Shawn stared at her, wearing a look of concern.

"I'm fine, Shawn. Really." Helesys walked past him, putting a hand on his shoulder as she passed. "You worried the magical fire will go out?"

Shawn walked behind her. "I can worry about both you and your spell, you know. Without you, it's just Taunauk to keep me warm." He chuckled nervously.

The three walked around the foot of the mountain in silence, eyes searching the stone face and the hills, lest more danger come for them.

Helesys couldn't help but think back to controlling the ray. She thought again of the Wolf King and of Sigun, and how easily they'd used such a spell. Did they feel the recoil as she had? Did it take a callous Terran to wield such power? Or did one merely become numb to it?

Either way, Helesys felt a sharp separation between herself and those tyrannical creatures. It was both an ideological and imposing line between them.

~ ~ ~

# The Hollows

The heroes walked around the edge of the Godpeak. Taunauk in front, Helesys in the middle, and Shawn behind. The weaver felt small, as if she were walking beside the infinite wall again. It wasn't so long ago that the weaver tried climbing its heights, only to succumb to exhaustion and plummet to her death.

But back then, at the edge of the wode, Helesys had been weaker, weary, and alone. She was none of those things now.

In the spots where the slope of the mountain was especially steep and close enough to touch, Helesys reached out and ran her thin metal fingers across the surface—gouging the ice, marring it. Answers loomed somewhere on the peak, somewhere lost in the cloud-covered sky, and this time, she would not be denied.

"Over here," Taunauk called over the wind.

He led them past an outcropping to a towering crevice. The opening was nearly ten feet across at the base, and stretched nearly up into the clouds, as if the mountain had been cleaved in two.

As they neared, Helesys felt the innate direction of her wand. "This is the way," she said. She held up her gauntlet and conjured her warding light.

The passage in front of them was short and triangular shaped. As the three passed through, the icy blue walls shimmered with her light and opened to a cavern beyond.

Shawn asked, "Does this seem strange to anyone else?" Helesys turned to see the rogue running a gloved hand over the ice. He added, "It's perfectly sheer. I remember seeing precision like this in the factory. Done by templates and simple machines. No Terran hand made this."

Taunauk continued through to the end of the passage, Everfall and axe in hand, but hanging at his side instead of at the ready. Helesys and Shawn followed, and the three emerged from the short tunnel.

The cavern before them was immense and intricate. A sloping staircase wrapped around the out wall, leading to dozens of small passages. Above them hung a web of icy paths and harsh shadows from Helesys's light.

From the heights came a melodious and haunting sound, one that seemed to rise and fall like the ebbing of waves.

"It's the wind," Helesys thought aloud. The ebb of the sound followed the gusts of wind from behind them.

"That's good," Shawn said. "I've had about my fill of monsters already."

Taunauk said, "We've only met one."

"Yeah, one from this realm. I still haven't forgotten about Mr. Mask, or the faceless people, or the aliens. What was before that? Oh yeah, murderous automatons—Yeah, I could go with a nice, *cold*, boring mountain."

Helesys replied, "You still haven't learned about giving breath to fate."

"How's a Terran supposed to comment on his existential place in the world without doing that?"

She and Taunauk shared a smirk, and the weaver led them up the outer staircase. They climbed the stairs in silence, their footsteps and the melodious song the only accompaniment. Helesys imagined that Shawn was second guessing his monologue.

As they ascended, they passed mottled outcroppings of dark stone and jagged sections that seemed to rise from the depths of the ice like a creature just barely beneath the waves. It wasn't until they passed a reptilian skull embedded just beneath the ice, that Helesys realized they were bones.

Stranger still were the divots and pockmarks on the stairs. Helesys stooped down to examine these. There was no trace of magic, but when she looked upward, she found similar tiny blemishes on the ceiling—as if something had dripped or melted through.

The air grew chill as they ascended, and with it, the latent feeling of magic grew. It felt like walking into mist.

"That's an unpleasant feeling," Shawn said from behind.

"Indeed," Taunauk grumbled. "It is *old* magic, like that of the god serpent."

Helesys thought on this. "Wherever it came from… it is so old that it is a remnant of what it once was, and it was immensely powerful for its echo to be felt so." She jested, "Especially for a barbarian and a rogue to feel it."

"Hardy har har," Shawn replied, pushing playfully on her shoulder.

Taunauk was silent a moment longer before replying seriously. "She has a point. Perhaps that is why the spirits are said to congregate on the mountain."

And with that, the seriousness of the moment was back. Helesys shook her head.

They came to the first junction midway up the stairs and paused. They could continue up the stairs to any number of honeycomb passages, but Helesys felt the guidance of her wand-arm urging her through the closest narrow passageway in the wall.

Then came her wand's quiet internal voice: *This is a resonating chamber. The mountain seems to be full of them.*

*Like a musical instrument?* Helesys asked.

*Or like an item imbued with magic. Some of the larger machines from Novissimé were made this way. Forged with pockets and channels for magic.*

Helesys looked upon the mountain with renewed wonder. "Shawn's right," she said aloud. She told Taunauk and Shawn of the resonating chambers. "Someone or something made this place. Perhaps they merely carved these passages for a purpose."

Taunauk asked, "Did your wand tell you that?"

"Yes."

The barbarian nodded thoughtfully. "I wonder if you'll find it easier to communicate with your wand in a place like this."

*Perhaps*, her wand said. Helesys echoed the word aloud.

~

The narrow passage stretched on. The icy walls shimmered with warding light and carried the haunting melody of the wind.

Taunauk was walking in front when the Endroggen paused in the tunnel. He knelt to examine the floor.

"Blood," he said plainly.

After he stood and continued walking, Helesys stooped to the same spot. She saw tiny, frozen droplets of red—so small that she would've missed them had it not been for his observation.

Taunauk gestured to the wall farther down, noting more blood—several streaks. Helesys imagined Terran fingers leaving trails across the frozen wall.

Helesys didn't need the warning of her wand to begin kindling power in her gauntlet and strength in her body, unsure of which she would need. Meanwhile, she kept a hold on the warmth for her and Shawn. She breathed a sigh of concentration and relief—at the moment, maintaining the balance for just herself and Shawn was a much easier task than it had been with so many survivors on the hills.

"Something foul lurks here," Shawn muttered. The quivering in his voice made Helesys think the rogue could feel it, too.

The blood increased as they pressed on through the tunnel, turning to trails and splatters of frozen red. They passed handprints on the floor. Each had five fingers, but they were large and elongated. The weaver's mind drifted back to the dancer they'd encountered in the dumbwaiter to the wizard's tower. Long-limbed and spider-like, with dead eyes and drooling tongue. It was the face that made Helesys shiver—the face Helesys had seen so clearly when she'd used her holding spell on the creature.

Whatever creature waited for them now in the icy halls wasn't the dancer—that thought alone reassured her. The dancer was a made-thing, something created by Amadeus himself. She would not see its like in this frozen place.

But as the heroes emerged from the tunnel into the next large, resonating chamber, Helesys's mind raced. The chamber stretched upward in a conic shape. More honeycomb passages branched away at different heights—

And all the room was caked in blood. So much was haphazard smears and speckles, but there were three sections that took the form of crude red paintings.

Distinct, thick trails led from the floor to the upper passageways, as if the creature that lived there had dragged its wounded prey up to feast in privacy.

Shawn whispered, "What do we do?"

Helesys searched her wand's direction and turned toward one of the ground-level passages—one of the least blood-covered. She pointed toward it.

The three turned so that they were back-to-back, facing outward with weapons drawn while they shuffled toward the passage, their eyes scanning the chamber from top to bottom.

They were nearly across when Shawn whispered again, "I see it."

Taunauk muttered, "There is more than one."

Helesys saw nothing on her side, and so quickly glanced in both of their directions.

Ghoulish Terran faces peered down at them from the highest tunnels. Their eyes were wide and lidless, their jaws were elongated so that their lips didn't cover the red and purple-stained teeth. Their hair was long and patchy, and clung frozen to the sides of their faces.

Taunauk said, "To the tunnel!"

But as they turned to run, another of the ghoulish Terrans appeared at the end of the tunnel. It was hunched, walking with folded bat-like limbs, and staring at Helesys. The next moment, it was lumbering down the tunnel on long limbs, its mouth opened so wide it looked like the jaw was melting. It didn't scream or cry—it charged with only the horrid scraping sound of nails on the ice.

The heroes stopped at the edge of the tunnel, and Helesys called on the Ring of Winter, channeling its power into her gauntlet. She fired half a dozen icy blasts at the edges of the tunnel. These struck and formed growths of ice that sealed the tunnel—nearly. The creature slammed into the ice with a pitiful thump, then snaked a long arm through the cracks. Ice gouged its skin and the arm flailed wildly, reaching nearly ten feet past the ice.

Back in the chamber, four more of the creatures lurked in the high tunnels, peering over the edge. Then they lumbered down the walls like giant spiders.

Helesys turned her gauntlet toward them and fired several shots, but the long-limbed creatures jerked their bodies out of the way with supernatural quickness.

"Come on then!" Taunauk roared and beat his shield and axe together. Meanwhile, gray mist rose from Shawn's head and shoulders as the rogue called on his mysterious power.

"Kill them quick!" Helesys shouted, then churned power and uttered the holding spell. "*Restu sonmova, lamia.*"

The ghoulish Terrans froze in their twisted strides, the scraping stopped and silence fell over the scene.

~

The world fell away and Helesys awoke in another version of the icy cavern—the shared mindspace of the holding spell.

For a breath, Helesys was alone. The chamber appeared to be the same as before, except that there appeared to be no blood. She looked around and decided it was completely clean.

Then Helesys saw movement in the tunnel. Terrans—wounded elves and humans—limping through the passage toward her. Helesys stepped aside and watched as the group of six shuffled past her and slumped down against the frozen wall. They carried torches and spears, and spoke the common tongue—though it was wrought with words she didn't recognize and her wand-arm hummed intermittently with translation.

"Do you *think* we lost it *back there?*" one of the wounded elves asked. She clutched at her side with both hands.

"Silence," another elf said as he tended her wound. His hair was long, braided, and matted with snow. "That *doesn't matter.* We need to *see to* your wound."

Two of the human men watched the tunnel with spears at the ready. "I *think* we're safe," one whispered. The tips of their spears glistened red in the torchlight.

Minutes stretched on and no one spoke.

Helesys paced idly, her eyes darting from opening to opening—waiting. Every other time she'd used the holding spell, she'd been placed in a psychic struggle against the target, but this felt different. It reminded her of how she'd peered into the memory glass aboard the Idnauthi ship and watched the life of Sigun. She'd lived years of the alien's life in flashes of minutes.

The walls shimmered, and all at once, the Terrans reappeared around the room. Most stood in different positions, save for the wounded elven woman. She lay in the same slumped pose in the corner. Her breathing was shallow.

Helesys decided that she was looking at a memory… but *whose* memory?

"We press on," one of the men said. He knocked the butt of his spear against the ice for effect. "We make it to the summit. There has to be something there."

"No," the elf with braided hair said. "We are *waiting* right here. The *second party* will come for us. *Another* day, at most." He stooped beside the wounded elf and brushed the hair affectionately from her face.

"You're all mad," the first man replied, before storming down the passage. Another Terran reluctantly followed.

Helesys watched them leave, then turned back to the scene. The torches still burned just as they had before, without wear or dwindling. She watched one human pull a strip of jerky from his pack. After a moment, he offered it to the braided elf.

"You need to *eat something.*"

"But that's… how *much* do we *have left?*"

"That's it," the man whispered. "*Gods* help us."

Time jumped, and again the group were standing in different positions. Now the wounded elf was slumped over on the floor while the other elf sat quietly beside her—his eyes were bloodshot and frozen tears marred his cheeks.

The six that were left huddled together for warmth, clutching their stomachs. Their gazes strayed to the fallen elf and lingered on her frozen body.

The cavern blurred, and Helesys saw the elf with the braided hair kneeling overtop of the fallen. Bending over and cutting at her frozen arm. The cloth came away in chunks that were hurriedly cast aside. The others in the group watched, hands to their mouths in shock. But as they watched and their faces turned in disgust, they slid slowly across the ice as if pulled by the cannibalistic scene.

Even then, Helesys thought she could see the face of the elf changing. The icy blood on his mouth grew warm and dripped down his chin, seemingly to elongate his face with it.

Her wand whispered, *Such a gruesome act in such a magic laden place changed them. Wendigo is the old word for what they have become— Helesys, the memory is fading!*

The cavern was already blurred, and now the Terrans disappeared too. Helesys felt dizzy with vertigo.

~

Helesys bolstered her strength, fighting to stay conscious, and the world came back to her. The Wendigos stuttered as they clung to the walls, but now lumbered forward.

It was as if only a breath had passed since she attempted the holding spell. The long minutes watching the exploring party nearly freeze and then succumb to cannibalism—nothing more than fleeting memory.

Taunauk roared and slashed at the first Wendigo to touch the floor. The creature was still dazed from Helesys's spell, and the barbarian's axe cleaved it in half from shoulder across its ribs. The head and left arm fell to the ice, but the creature still thrashed.

Shawn's foe recovered quicker, and as the rogue slashed at it with brilliant daggers, the creature twisted and contorted itself in attempt to bite him. Even as the wounds on its body grew innumerable, the creature did not slow or seem to notice at all.

Another Wendigo leapt from the upper passages, easily clearing the room, and landed snarling beside the weaver. Helesys turned and split power between her body, the gauntlet, and the Gar of Shéslang. She lashed out with the staff, spinning it and batting away the long, grisly fingers of the Wendigo, and filling the space between with blasts from her wand-arm. But even as her frenzy grew and looked like Helesys would over-shadow the snarling creature, still the Wendigo fought. Even her power could not turn it aside.

*You must burn them, Helesys. We know the spell.*

Helesys felt it, as surely as she had felt the grisly flashback of the Wendigos. A spell dredged up from the abyss of memory in a time of need. A suddenly remembered dream.

*"Immotalem Immortalis!"*

Helesys brought her metal hand to her face and felt the magic course around her gauntlet. Then she released it as if she were blowing a kiss and breathed out. Fire blossomed from her breath, brilliant—nearly blinding—and washed over her enemy.

The Wendigo let out a guttural howl and cowered, shrinking into a crumpled, burning ball, before slumping silently against the wall.

The weaver recoiled from the flames. Even though she felt the warm swell of power in her chest, the flames were painfully hot as they left her mouth—even with kindled resilience.

Without pausing, Helesys turned the spell toward the others, shouting for Taunauk to get back, and then Shawn. The injured Wendigos fought with hunger and bloodlust, and paid no mind to the fellows as they were burned, one by one.

And when those in the cavern were folded and burning, Helesys turned to the Wendigo still trapped in the narrow passageway. It thrashed a solitary arm through the ice-blocked passage. Helesys breathed fire and moments later it was silent, still wedged in the ice cracks like a burning marionette.

"That was convenient," Shawn said, slipping daggers back into his ethereal pouch. "Necessity is the mother of invention, or something like that."

"I knew a great many spells. I just can't remember them all." Helesys released the fire magic, and then the bolstering spells—save for kindled warmth. She breathed a sigh of relief. She looked upon the smoldering corpses with reluctance.

"What's the matter?" Taunauk asked. "Is it the fire spell?"

Helesys shook her head. "The fire wasn't pleasant, but it worked. No. It's just... *I saw them*. They were elven and human—just exploring, as we are." She explained their cannibalism and the curse that resulted from it.

Shawn chuckled nervously. "And we're sure that we want answers from this place? What if we don't like what we find out?"

"I would rather know," Taunauk said sternly.

A moment later, Helesys and Shawn muttered in agreement. They had come far—they would not be turned now.

~ ~ ~

# The Throat of the Mountain

The heroes pressed further into the hollow of the Godpeak, eager to leave fresh carnage behind them. Helesys's wand-arm led them up another three icy flights and through several more passages before the three sought to rest. Again they saw the tiny blemishes—of drippings from the ceiling—heavy sprinklings in some areas and absent in others.

They had found a second large, open chamber. The walls of which were embedded with giant birds. Most of the creatures vanished beneath the frosty depths; All that was near enough the surface were the outline of wings with flight feathers nearly twenty feet long.

The heroes slumped against the wall beneath one such wing.

"Are you sure this is a good place to stop?" Shawn asked.

"As good a place as any," Helesys replied. "My wand is silent."

Shawn gave a small nod, and the three of them opened their pouches of lichen and snowberries from the Lamoral. Helesys bowed her head and spoke the words of the *Baccanova* spell as she'd learned from Emilee.

For a moment, Shawn pulled out a ration of jerky, then stuffed it back in his pack. "I don't have the stomach for it. Nothing that used to have a face. Nothing smoked either."

Helesys was the first to eat. She chewed slowly, savoring the taste.

Shawn asked tentatively, "What does it taste like?"

It took her a moment to realize what he was asking, for he'd already tried some in the village. "It doesn't taste any different with the spell."

For a time, they ate in silence, and Helesys's thoughts drifted back to the Wendigos and the memory she had seen. The creatures had been so similar to the dancer in the dumbwaiter. Helesys was certain that Amadeus had seen them before and used them for inspiration. How had she been able to hold that creature and not the Wendigos?

Her wand said, *One cannot bind a creature such as that for long, no matter how powerful the mage. It is not a made-thing, it is a curse.*

*What about the memory I saw?*

*An effect of the mountain. The same magic that causes spirits to congregate here and allows the mortal to speak with them.*

*Something else that's been bothering me,* Helesys replied. *Why are there spirits in the dungeon? In a place where they cannot die?*

*Sublimation. It is like O'Ten said. One lives so long that they begin to forget. Think of the lost civilizations you've seen. Just because a Terran cannot die doesn't mean that eventually it won't be eroded by time.*

Helesys pondered this. Her mind stretched and tried to grasp such a concept as *deep time*. Did a Terran eventually stop reincarnating in this place? How long would it take? How many lifetimes would one live and suffer? And then what happened to the souls here?

But it was too big an idea, and the weaver stopped trying to grasp the concept. If the heroes had their way, she would not be there long enough for it to matter.

~

Taunauk broke the silence of the cavern.

"I was quick to answer when you asked about Endroggen rage. It is blood magic, as I said, but perhaps the metaphor of a bottled storm is not enough.

"Anyone can harbor violence. Anyone can seek vengeance. In anger, a man could pick up a chunk of iron and beat another with it—they may even kill without meaning to. In vengeance, a man might trade for a dagger, plan revenge, and wait for the perfect moment to strike. Then slit their enemy's throat. But what of the soldier who practices violence against an opponent they have never met, or might never meet?

"Endroggen rage is none of those things. Those things alone are not enough.

"To be Endroggen is to become a blacksmith. To work emotion as they work metal. To take the harmless chunk of iron and forge it into something greater. Heat it, hammer and shape it into a sword. Then to practice with the sword until the blade is an extension of the self, and violence becomes as easy as waking from a shallow sleep. Endroggen do this without ever knowing when we will meet our enemy or who they will be—only that the blade is with us, always; ready to wake us from shallow dream.

"We do this because our people have always done this. We are not warmongers, nor are we prone to violence amongst our own."

Taunauk punctuated the speech by eating another handful of food.

Helesys added, "You said, rage is shared only with the enemy."

Taunauk nodded slightly. "My father's words. My words. Rage is not only for weapons. It can be for tools, though I… I know little of this. There are Endroggen who use their blood magic to make art and smithery, or song that swell the breast, others that turn it to a lover's passion. Purest emotion channeled into many things…"

Shawn asked with a mouthful of food, "Why didn't you ever use it like that?"

"…The more I remember about my life and about my people, I feel that much of that world was lost to me."

Helesys recalled Taunauk's title of Aonar. That he thought himself clanless.

Instead of asking more, Helesys merely said, "We will reach the peak, and we will find answers."

Shawn added, "Godsdamnright we will."

~

Ever upward they walked, across the pockmarked floors of chambers and passages that grew ever wider.

"Does that seem strange to you?" Shawn asked quietly. He pointed to the widening passage. "Shouldn't things be getting smaller as we reach the peak?"

Taunauk grumbled from in front. "The marks on the floor and ceiling are growing larger."

Helesys eyed the walls and found similar divots on the bottom sections—around those marks on the floor.

"Splash marks," she mumbled. "Something has melted through the ceiling, fallen to the floor, and splashed across the lower walls."

"Good to know," Shawn muttered, his eyes wearily scanning the passage ceiling.

"They're old here," Helesys added. "The ice across the ceiling has refrozen. You can't see completely through it."

"Quiet," Taunauk said, slowing. He pointed to the end of the passage, to the next chamber. "Do you see it?"

At the end of the passage, Helesys saw the intermittent flash of orange—the dripping of something molten. Wisps of steam punctuated each drop.

Helesys's wand-arm hummed with warning. Again, she kindled power and strength.

They pressed forward silently, and came to a cavern at the end of the passage. Drops of glowing orange fell steadily in the center of the room. The floor was gouged in those places and steam hung thin in the air. Huge boulders of ice littered the room in the spaces inbetween.

Above them, the center of the ceiling was completely melted, and Helesys saw vaguely into the next cavern beyond. It was cloaked in darkness and steam, but there was a subtle blue glow, punctuated by lines of sweltering orange.

And the thing moved.

From the darkness, dozens of glistening white eyes blinked in discordant time. The blue unraveled, becoming thick coils of chitin—the chinks between the plates blazed and dripped molten orange to the floor. As the creature moved, it belched steam down into their lower cavern.

A jagged head lowered through the broken ceiling, wide and frilled, with twitching mandibles. Now Helesys saw it clearly: The long, powerful body, and many jagged legs. A giant centipede that was neither ice nor fire, but some vicious combination of both.

Its many eyes scanned the room, settled on the heroes, and then narrowed at Helesys.

*It can sense magic,* her wand said. *It knows you're a weaver.*

Helesys grit her teeth. *It will regret going for the weaver first,* she replied.

The centipede's mouth opened, revealing hundreds of needle-sharp teeth. Instead of snarling, the orange glow grew brilliant—like fire welled in its throat and in between its joints. The molten liquid fell in steady drips and sizzled on the floor.

Helesys leveled her gauntlet and fired. Her warding light shrank and purple arcane energy tore across the cavern. The creature recoiled from the blasts, two of which struck chitin and flared into a shower of sparks. The walls trembled and sharp cracks echoed from its many jabbing steps as it retreated back into the darkness of the higher chamber.

Vicious echoes sounded above them, and the ceiling began to quake. Then came two horrid cracks and the sound of paper tearing as the ice above them gave way. Helesys, Taunauk, and Shawn dove for safety and slid across the ice.

The collapse sounded like thunder, and an icy blast washed over the room. Helesys pushed herself up from the floor and opened her eyes to find the centipede standing over the rubble. Taunauk and Shawn were already on their feet, barbarian glowing golden and rogue with a wispy veil.

Taunauk and Shawn charged, while Helesys lashed out again with her gauntlet. The heroes met the beast with a hail of steel of magic.

The centipede lunged for Shawn, mouth gaping and trailing molten saliva, but the rogue was far too quick. He stepped out of the way, leaving nothing but an afterimage in his wake. Shawn ran around and leapt to the back of its head, trying to slip his blades between its plates.

Meanwhile, Taunauk stowed Everfall on his backsling, and leapt atop the writhing creature. It tried to throw him off, but he held on with one hand and struck with his axe.

Helesys bolstered her shots. Each slammed into the beast and caused it to tremble.

But nothing broke through the centipede's chitin armor—not arcane blast, Endroggen rage, or blur of speed. Nor could the creature shake the heroes' assault.

The orange gaps in its armor glowed bright. Steam billowed and the room grew hot. Shawn leapt away from the creature and landed near Helesys.

"It's like it's blood is boiling," Shawn said, breathing heavily. Helesys could feel the heat emanating from him.

Taunauk lasted only a few more moments, leaping from it and backing away. He pulled Everfall from his back and stood defiantly—even from across the room, Helesys could see that the blades of his axe were warped from the intense heat.

The monster opened its mouth and the brilliant orange seeped from it, dripping from between its needle teeth. Its face began to quiver violently and without noise, save for the rattling of its armor plates, as if the creature were about to charge—

A feeling of dread overcame the weaver, punctuated by a rattle of warning from her wand.

Helesys called upon the Ring of Winter, and as she stared down the centipede, she compounded the ring with power from the Gar of Shéslang.

*"Hieme Murum!"*

The tendril of ice and pain slithered from her nerves—her legs, her arms—pulled out in one violent yank. All at once, Helesys gasped and fell to one knee. She leaned heavy on the staff and fought for breath.

She willed the *Shield of Frost* forward instead of around her. The tendril of white began to lurch and lash like stuttered lightning, the cracks so frequent that the cavern became awash in light.

"To me!" she screamed to her comrades, for she knew what the monster was going to do—

But in the maelstrom, she couldn't find them.

The world grew orange, as if the sun had been brought to the tiny cavern, and the sound of lightning was eclipsed by roaring fire as the centipede spewed its molten breath across the room. A mass of fire slammed into the shield. Helesys had no idea how much was turned away, only that her muscles burned and her head pounded with effort, and that chunks of still-smoldering rock pelted the floor in front of her like rain.

Even behind the veil of frost, the weaver began to sweat and the air grew too painful to breathe. She felt the magic of the ring running out and the sound of molten rain growing. In one last gasp of power, she shouted, *"Frigus inspiratione!"*

The cracking whip of ice burst forth in a silent, violent attack. Even with her eyes closed and buried in the crook of her metal arm, the world was white and silent.

Helesys thought she'd died. She only knew otherwise when she felt the stuttering steps of the monster. She strained to open her eyes—to see the carnage wrought.

The cavern was covered in jagged boulders—a wreckage of ice and rock. Between the large masses were pebbles and sand—the remnants of the molten breath. The centipede reared back, towering over the scene. Its joints no longer burned with molten orange, now the creature was merely a glowing blue. Taunauk glowed golden, and he and his golden warriors slashed at the creature's legs and body. Shawn was a blur; he ran up the wall and leapt to the centipede's face, slashing at its eyes as it writhed.

And the mountain trembled beneath her knees. Still fighting for breath, Helesys looked around and saw splinters and cracks appearing in the floor.

Moments later, the floor collapsed, and the heroes and the monster fell.

~

Again, Helesys awoke deaf and in chaos. Her face was covered in frost and the cavern was filled with haze. She felt tremors in the ice beneath her—the jabbing legs of the centipede—and saw glimpses of its undulating body in the mist like a serpent beneath the waves.

In the surreal quiet, she felt thunderous cracks shake the mountain—far too powerful to be the centipede or remnants of her magic—and she feared the mountain might give way. She thought of the answers promised to them on the summit, and that they might be buried beneath them. Denied answers and sent wandering again.

Helesys searched for the small flame within her that bolstered warmth for her and Shawn, and shunted the rest of her power to her strength.

As she leaned on the spear and rose to her feet, the silence lifted. Breath and strength swelled within her, as if she'd woken from a dream. She heard the clangs of steel and chitin—cracks grew and splintered in the wall to her right. Again, she saw the giant buried wings of slumbering creatures buried beneath the ice. Had they really fallen so far through the mountain by the molten bleeding of the centipede?

Her question was cut short by an explosion. Helesys recoiled as the splintered wall burst outward. When she looked again, there was nothing but the swirling void of open air, of dark sky and howling wind—

And it shimmered.

For a breath, Helesys didn't know what she was looking at. Something massive stood where the broken wall used to—something transparent that blended into the void behind it.

It wasn't until the thing moved that Helesys truly saw it: An enormous owl freed from its icy imprisonment. It reached out with wings that stretched across the cavern, and Helesys watched as its wings showed first void and then ice as they passed in front of the cavern wall—only visible as it moved.

It paused like that, wings outstretched, its body leaning forward menacingly, and again it disappeared behind a clear veil. Meanwhile, the frantic battle in the room continued, her comrades little more than desperate blurs against the might of the centipede.

The owl pounced—a movement so fast and powerful that the mountain quaked beneath it. The flap of its wings picked Helesys up and threw her against the wall. Beyond the sudden pain, she heard two more impacts—her comrades tossed similarly.

When Helesys fell to the floor and opened her eyes, she saw a titanic struggle. The near-invisible owl stood over the writhing centipede, one set of enormous talons wrapped around the neck of its enemy. The centipede twitched and its mouth hung open in a silent scream. In spite of the monster's struggle, the owl moved only slightly to pin it down.

Taunauk and Shawn ran over to her.

Shawn asked, "What in Movernus's name is that?"

Taunauk grumbled, "For now, it is an ally."

Then the owl spoke in a haunting voice, like wind through a dead forest. "Be gone, Yhlesh. Before I eat you." And as it spoke, the head of the owl turned from clear to the color of cracked stone, like ink bleeding onto the page, before receding like a wave on the shore.

The centipede struggled viciously now; the lower half of it whipped around and its many legs jabbed desperately. Its mouth glowed orange and it sprayed its fire breath at the owl. Chunks of molten ichor landed on the invisible giant, and fell harmlessly to the floor.

"I said, be gone!"

The owl flapped its wings, and the heroes shielded themselves from the gusts. Then the giant lifted the centipede up and in one powerful motion, heaved it toward the nearest opening. The centipede crashed against the ice and then limped into the passageway—its chitin scraping the walls.

The giant owl turned to them, and even though its outline blended into the wall behind it, Helesys knew it was staring at them.

"Come with me, wanderers," it said, its face awash in gray. "Quickly, before Yhlesh returns. I will take you to the top of the mountain."

Helesys and Taunauk exchanged a glance, and before the weaver could ask if her comrades understood the giant, Shawn answered—

"Okay."

~

Before the Helesys or Taunauk could protest, the owl swept the heroes close and bid them hold onto its legs. Helesys and Shawn held to one, Taunauk to the other.

Though Helesys could only see the ghostly outline of the leg, she felt cold stone beneath her hands. She kept her kindled strength and warmth for her and Shawn, and held on tight. In one thunderous movement, the owl leapt through the shattered wall and into the wintery open air.

They climbed into the air, the owl's wings as silent as a specter, and soared. The realm stretched out beneath them, a blur of wind and white. The giant owl banked and rose to the top of the Godpeak.

Helesys gasped, for the mountain was awash in color—greens and reds and bright blue—and seemed to stretch upward forever. Yet now she could see the limits of it. She saw the taper of the slope, and then the peak itself, and in that moment, the mountain felt so very small.

They landed in a clearing—inconceivably close to the summit. Helesys guessed that now they were only a short hike from the peak.

The three heroes stepped back and craned their necks to look upon the giant owl. In the maelstrom, they could see the owl clearly—the whipping snow highlighting the owl, even as it stood motionless.

It stared back at them.

"Thank you," Helesys said.

And when it did not answer right away, Shawn asked, "So, are you going to tell us what you are? Or how you knew that we were going to the summit?"

"My name is Kuatari, and my kind are Resnocti, guardians of the wild, the grove, and the thicket." It spoke patiently, letting the ebbs of gray grow and diminish—only letting the color reach its shoulders. "I guessed you were going to the summit, for no traveler goes anywhere else."

Helesys said tentatively, "You're a long way from a forest."

"Indeed. That was before we were trapped here in the dungeon. We were guides and guardians of the forest once. Invisible and silent, even our words match those we speak to—but not even our gifts could hide us from the dungeon. After we were trapped, we wandered the realms, and when we grew tired, we made a nest in the mountain. When food grew scarce, we slept. Now It is only fitting that I guide when I can."

Shawn mumbled, "He wasn't kidding about eating that centipede."

"And I will," it replied, "before I sleep again. I will crack his chitin and feast on molten insides. Send Yhlesh wandering."

Helesys listened, but she was drawn back to what Kuatari had said…

"The dungeon wanders," Helesys said. "It has appeared in so many places, and trapped so many different creatures. In forests, underwater, in the sky, even in space. It must travel the real world somehow."

Kuatari said, "It is fitting that a wandering prison would strive to make wanderers of us all."

The Resnocti turned to leave. Helesys wanted to ask it to stay. They had so many questions.

It was Taunauk who spoke. "Kuatari, we are chosen. We can bring back treasure after death. We seek the death of the Wolf King. Have you ever met others like us?"

Kuatari paused and swiveled its head backward to them. "I have met two other groups of chosen."

Then the owl leapt into the air, shaking the ice beneath their feet. As it disappeared into the maelstrom, its haunting voice called back to them.

"The Wolf King still lives."

~ ~ ~

# The Godpeak

The three walked abreast the short way to the summit. The air was thin and biting, and Helesys found that she kindled breath as well as warmth. Snow swirled around their feet.

In view now, was the frosty summit of the Godpeak—no wider across than the caverns had been. The maelstrom seemed slow here, and snowy clouds gave way to starry night sky and brilliant, swirling color. Streams of green, deep reds and electric blues danced in the sky, like light shimmering in glass.

She could see movement within those swathes of colors, like fish darting just beneath the surface of water.

"Wait," Taunauk said. He stopped and pointed down to the realm beneath.

They shouldn't have been able to see the landscape—it should've been veiled behind perpetual winter storms. Helesys saw across the tapestry of the realm: A world in swathes of whites, browns, and greens, marred by deep gashes and ridges—

And as she stared, Helesys saw a pattern. It was something akin to script, though neither she nor her wand recognized the language. Everywhere she looked, she saw the realm writ large in script, letters connecting to one another with purpose— completely surrounding the Godpeak.

"There is lingering magic here," Helesys said, musing aloud. "Echoes of magic. The resonating chambers in the mountain, and now this." She pointed to the script embedded in the landscape. "Something *made* this place."

Shawn coughed. "I mean, this place is definitely *something*. I can feel the energy here. It's unlike anything I've… But someone *making* this place? That's crazy. … Right?"

The weaver shook her head. "Something either carved the landscape or… By Movernus, maybe they blasted it away, like an artist working stone, cleaving and scraping it away. I don't know…"

Helesys's eyes followed the script as close to the mountain as she could without peering over. And as her eyes fell, she saw Taunauk's axe. The blade was warped and scorched black— the runic engravings gone.

"Taunauk…"

"It is nothing."

"It's not *nothing*," she replied.

Taunauk said plainly, "The axe isn't magical, like Everfall. So it can be warped and broken."

He held up the axe, and Helesys heard Shawn wince behind her.

Taunauk sighed. "You're right. It was my father's axe, and I will carry it as long as I can—till it is shattered or splintered. In time, it will be nothing more than rage. All things are like that, destined to be only memories in those that follow us."

The aurora in the sky flared brightly and cast dazzling colors upon the snow.

The heroes shielded their eyes, and Helesys felt a great calling—not just the magic guidance of her wand, but a swelling in her chest. The peak was calling to them—

Something at the peak was calling to them.

Glowing figures appeared in the snow, many wearing fur, with long braided hair and beards.

Beside her, Taunauk dropped his weapons in the snow. Then he sprinted toward the figures.

Helesys stooped down, grabbed Everfall and the axe, and then her and Shawn followed with tentative excitement.

And as they ran, Helesys saw a small glowing child running beside the barbarian. Both Taunauk and the child stopped in front of the nearest figure—both fell to one knee.

Helesys and Shawn stopped and stood to the side.

The glowing man stood tall and strong. He was clad in Endroggen furs and leathers. Beneath his long hair and braided beard, she saw Taunauk's eyes and face staring back—the resemblance clear. He leaned on the pommel of an axe, the same as Taunauk's—unmarred.

The glowing boy shifted and changed between its small stature and that of a young man. Though the figure was young in each image, his head and face were always shaved. Even though Helesys had never seen the young visions before, she recognized her comrade in both.

Beside the boy, the real Taunauk wept quietly. His voice was harsh, the words hard fought.

"Rehkoros, Father, forgive me," Taunauk said. "I was born blind in this world and forgot my task."

"Rise, balac, and never kneel again."

Both Taunauk and his echo stood. The young looked up at the elder, while the man stood shoulder to shoulder with his father.

Rehkoros said, "You have found us, and for now, that is enough." His father's voice was stoic and warm and quelled the son's breath.

Taunauk looked at the dozens of Endroggen spirits on the peak. Each stared back at him.

"I don't understand," Taunauk said. "How are you here? You were already dead. I remember. You should be in Accaelum, the resting place of all our people."

"What have you learned about this place?"

"The dungeon is a soul trap. It has imprisoned countless beings—Terrans and gods alike. In the real world, it wanders from place to place. The only escape is through the Wolf King."

His father nodded. "And what would happen if such a monster wandered to Accaelum?"

Taunauk's eyes widened.

"Hear me, balac. Do you remember why you are Aonar?"

"No," Taunauk replied, trepidation on his face.

"Memories are echoes, balac. Events so strong that we carry their ripples wish us into the future. But some events are so strong that they are not just felt in the future, but in the past, as well. These echoes are omens of tragedy to come. We have felt such omens before wars and famine and times of untold suffering, perhaps once a generation one is felt... But we had never felt something so grave as this. A blight upon Accaelum. Ten thousand souls devoured." Rehkoros suppressed a shiver and continued.

"In omens past, an Endroggen is called forth to be a champion of our people. A symbol to rally behind. But the elders needed more."

Rehkoros stepped forward and placed a hand on his son's shoulder. In that moment, it seemed as if the elder diminished; that Taunauk stood even taller.

"The elders chose you. You were taught and molded to be the strongest of us, the best with a blade. You were forbidden from ever being one of us. From playing, from loving.

"This time, the Endroggen needed a champion *and a vessel.* A warrior that could find the trapped souls of our people. One that could bind them and carry them within. That could save them from the dungeon—bring them home. That is why you are here.

"You were born into this world Aonar, so that you could become the vessel. It is I who asks forgiveness, Taunauk. You were denied so much." Rehkoros's face twisted in pain, and his hand fell from his son, but Rehkoros's voice was firm. "The elders did this. *I did this.*"

Helesys had been spellbound, and she did not see Taunauk's gaze fall. His eyes were closed, head hung.

"I forgive you, father." Taunauk's words were dutiful—measured and cold as stone.

Silence fell, and for a moment there was nothing but the cold, thin air between them, but it might as well have been a chasm.

Pain left Rehkoros's face and Taunauk met his eyes.

"I haven't found the other lost souls yet," Taunauk said, his voice wavering.

"You will." Then Rehkoros turned to Helesys and held out his hand. "My son's axe, please." She lay Everfall in the snow, walked over and presented the axe.

Rehkoros grasped the warped axe in one hand, then picked up his own spectral axe with the other.

"You may be Aonar, but you will never walk alone. We are all that made it to the Godpeak, but we will join you, walk beside you, and fight beside you. When you have need of us, you will find our strength. Our rage is yours."

Then Rehkoros brought the two axes together, melding them in a quiet, glowing power. When the flare passed, he was holding a single axe—Taunauk's axe. The blade was reformed and the runes glowed with a smoldering of ghostly power.

"My blade is yours."

He presented the axe, and Taunauk received it, glancing at it for only a moment before letting it hang at his side.

Taunauk stared at his father, emotion swelling behind his stoic facade.

"If I find the other Endroggen, If we escape. I know what will happen… All their souls will be free. You will leave me."

"Yes, balac. As all fathers one day leave their sons."

"Then I shall miss you."

"And I, you." Again, Rehkoros's hand fell to his son's shoulder. "Have you felt my strength in your rage?"

"Only when needed, athair."

"Does my hand guide your hand?"

"Not since I was a boy."

"Because you do not need it. You must trust in yourself. Trust that you will find the path just as you trust in your swordhand.

"Do not burden yourself with echoes and memories. They should strengthen us, not weigh upon us—a reassuring hand upon our shoulder. The warm weight of a cloak. Fond memories, not goodbyes."

Taunauk held his axe between them, and both he and Re-hkoros gripped the pommel. Together, father and son bowed their heads, and they said, "The blade holds the warrior as much as he holds the blade."

And as they shared the moment, the Endroggen souls walked across the snow, leaving no footprints. They came to Taunauk and gathered around him. They glowed and then disappeared, like snuffed candle flames—Rehkoros was last.

Then Taunauk stood alone. From his eyes came a bright golden glow—beams of light—that receded until there was only a flicker of color that should not be.

~

Taunauk stood alone in the snow, holding the faintly glowing axe. Helesys and Shawn stood in respectful silence.

It was a long moment before the Endroggen turned and looked at them; the axe fell to his side. Confusion, anger, and stoicism flashed across his face like flickering light.

"Attend to your own echoes," Taunauk said. His voice was pained. He turned and knelt in the snow, axe across his thighs. Discordant voices overlapped his own. *"The memories come for you."*

Shawn stepped forward to go to him, but Helesys grabbed his arm. "Give him a minute—"

An elven girl ran past them. Walls rose up around—a hallway with high, vaulted ceilings. The girl trailed her fingers along the wall as she went.

Helesys knew it was her own memory.

"Go," Shawn said softly. She didn't turn.

Helesys followed the girl down the hall. Her own fingers mirrored the girls', metal fingers finding no resistance.

Young Helesys wore a brilliant green dress laced with serpents, the snakes of Great House Byyra. Her long white hair billowed as she ran.

They came to a bedroom that Helesys knew to be her mother's. It would've overlooked the city of Novissimé, but drapes of teinlinen hung across the windows, casting the room in a dim red. All around the room were runes and the old words carved into the walls, the ceiling, and the floor. A large bed made of elderwood sat in the center, the history of House Byyra wrapped around the four tall posts.

Her mother, Wynbella, sat on the edge of the bed and beckoned Young Helesys over. She sat on the bed in front of her mother while Wynbella brushed the girl's long white hair.

Helesys watched spellbound, feeling both fond warmth and a pang of jealousy. She ran her elven hand through her own hair and felt it short—it only appeared long by illusion. She ended the spell. It was scarcely enough to brush; the hair did not touch her shoulder.

Young Helesys asked, "Why don't you have the curtains open, mother?"

"I don't want to. Not today."

"Will you come to the smithery with me today? I want to see what Professor Edmond is working on."

Wynbella hesitated, her lips twisting as if to say again, *not today*, but she stopped and forced a smile. "Ask me again after your lessons."

The young girl couldn't see Wynbella's struggle, not while Wynbella worked her hair… But Helesys knew—she had always known. That was why Helesys went to her so many times when the drapes were pulled and the room was dim. She still needed her mother, and she knew that her mother needed her as well.

The light of illusion flickered and years passed before Helesys's eyes. Wynbella's bedroom was the same, but now two women sat upon the bed.

And Helesys gasped.

It had only been ten years or twenty—Helesys was grown and only a shade younger than she was now, but Wynbella had aged too. Elves lived for a thousand years or more, and so the time should've been inconsequential for Wynbella, like the passing of a single year for a human.

Yet her mother was weary, and even in the dim light of the bedroom, Helesys could see that those few years had not been kind to Wynbella.

The scene alternated: Wynbella gently working Helesys's long white hair, and then daughter returning the favor.

It was during this second instance that her mother finally spoke. "If it were not for you and your sister, I fear this life would be a curse." Wynbella chuckled—painful and pitiful.

"Some days with Aradi, it is a curse."

"You don't mean that."

Helesys did, but the echo of her stayed silent as she worked her mother's hair.

"It's not fair to live so many years without him and to have so many more to come." There was a crack in her mother's voice, a single note that belied the pain. Somehow, that was all, and it brought back Helesys's memory of losing her father.

Helesys's echo struggled for words, and in the end she said, "The humans are not burdened like we are." And in her heart she meant, *I miss him too.*

Wynbella said, "There's a nobility in it—in a short life. We live so long we truly think that we have forever. We don't, Helesys. We don't."

The scene changed again.

Her mother's bedroom fell away, leaving only the Godpeak—only the snow and the biting wind.

Wynbella stood, hands clasped, eyes wrinkled in concern. "We've missed you so, Come back home where you belong. You don't have to fight anymore. You've sacrificed enough, haven't you?" Wynbella said, gesturing toward the metal arm.

Helesys stepped forward to hug her mother, but heard the quiet voice of her wand. *She's not here. She's only a memory.*

Helesys stopped mid-step, hands clenched.

And instead, she heard another voice—*her own voice*, echoing in the memory.

"*The war has taken everything from me,*" the echo said. "*There is nothing left!*" Anger seethed from the memory. The words felt as if they came from Helesys's own mouth. The words seethed with anger, and Helesys recoiled as if her lips had touched poison—

Her mother's face twisted into a mirror of Helesys's, both in shock at what the memory of Helesys had said.

Helesys reached out, metal hand trembling, stammering to apologize. How could she say such things to her mother? Helesys had felt nothing but warmth for Wynbella, and the echo of the poisonous words made her stomach turn.

Then Wynbella disappeared, and was replaced with Helesys's sister, Aradi. That familiar, disdainful smirk.

"I told you she wouldn't understand. How could she? She refused to see you; did you know that? They brought your mangled body in—so scorched she couldn't bear to look at you.

"But I stayed with you as they nursed you back to health." A flicker of seriousness passed over Aradi's face. "Don't *ever* forget that."

A metal hand reached out and seized Aradi by the throat. Helesys had been about to do the same, and glanced down at her own metal hand to see it clenched and at her side.

The echo held Aradi by the throat. *"One good deed does not undo a lifetime of lies."*

Aradi smiled—just smiled. Her teeth bared like a viper clutched too far down the neck.

"Two good deeds, sister. I found what you were looking for."

Then the memories disappeared in the snow.

~

Helesys breathed deep and steadied herself, frozen tears on her face. She turned and found Shawn staring up at the colors dancing in the sky.

She stepped toward him, and he addressed her without looking.

"The stars are a lie," he said. "I felt it on the *Malorienta*, then after the Idnauthi ship, as surely as I feel it here. Sigun and the rest of those poor bastards are up there now. So certain of themselves and they're hurtling toward a lie."

Shawn turned to her with the dancing lights reflected in his eyes. "What if we're wrong about the Wolf King? What if we're wrong about finding freedom?"

Helesys wanted to say that they had no other choice, but instead she breathed deep and measured, and searched for the words.

"The likes of so many cannot be wrong," she finally said. "One-Mind, Shéslang, Amadeus… I have faith in our course.

"What memories did you find here?" she asked.

Shawn turned again to the sky. "Do you remember when you peered into the mind of Mr. Mask?"

Helesys stepped closer in the snow. "Yes. I remember hearing your voice among the millions. Was I in your mind too?"

Shawn shook his head. "I could feel them—all of them—dormant, buried, and dreaming. That's how I felt them; they were dreaming of their old lives. That's how I felt you, too. You know, when Mr. Mask showed us those images of our past, he wasn't lying to us. That boy from my memory... I think Mr. Mask could see our pasts even better than we could."

The rogue hung his head. "There should've been another way out of that realm. All those souls, they'd found their pasts and their memories. That's how Mr. Mask kept them docile—he kept them dreaming."

"We did what we had to do," Helesys replied. Her face wrinkled in confusion. "What's all this about dreams, Shawn? This isn't the first time you've mentioned them."

"You're right." Shawn winced and smirked. "I'm neither man nor elf. Immune to most psychics. Wrought iron pains me. We kept thinking I was a wind elemental. But I remember now..."

Shawn removed his furs and his thin cloak, revealing a leather vest and strips of black cloth wound around his arms. He grasped the ends of the strips and began to unwind them.

As the wrappings came unbound, a ghostly haze emanated from him, and grew with each passing second.

The wrappings fell, and Shawn smoldered in white smoke as if the whole of him was aflame. He looked up at Helesys—His eyes were pools of void with green lights floating in the center.

Helesys stepped back, power kindled by reflex. "I don't understand."

"The cold doesn't hurt anymore," he said, smiling, void floating from his lips. "In fact, it feels like home… I am a wisp, Helesys. A wisp from the plane of dreams. My kind walk through the dreams of humans and elves, while being neither.

"I always knew I was different. I just never knew *what* I was."

"How can that be?" Helesys asked. "What about the grandfather and the boy, and the factory? You had a life. *A Terran life.*"

Shawn looked at his hands—whether at the smoke or the Terran form beneath, Helesys did not know. The rogue shook his head.

"I left the realm of dreams to live as a mortal, and sometime after that, I left the factory. What a fool I must've been to give up two lives." Again he smirked painfully. "No happy Terrans wander these realms, right?"

The smoke grew from Shawn, hiding his Terran outline completely. The wind on the Godpeak blew fierce.

"Do you know what this mountain is, Helesys?" Shawn called over the wind. "It isn't a soul well or a trap like the dungeon. I can hear them. Souls *choose* to come here."

Shawn became a billowing mist, and even the glow of his eyes became faint. His voice grew stoic and wondrous, and the rogue held out his arms. "Do you see me, Helesys? I *am* flying."

Before Helesys could reach for him, Shawn disappeared— lost in the wind.

Shawn was gone. She could no longer feel him. Her kindled warmth was for her and her alone. She yelled for him, and her anguish felt small compared to the mountain and the forces set against her.

Helesys looked out over the swirling landscape, ignoring the colors above and the remnants of magic writ large across the land. Her hands were clenched, fingernails digging into her palm and metal groaning.

"Damn you," she whispered to the dungeon, the King, the Gatekeeper, and any other that was listening.

Yet, she felt something… another echo, perhaps. Something that told her that no matter how far Shawn had gone, that he would return. And that was solace enough for now. She would see him again.

~

Helesys turned into the cold wind of the mountain and found Taunauk walking toward her.

Whatever turmoil the barbarian had felt, his face had returned to the same stoic front that she had come to know. Though she wanted to ask how he was doing, something told her that her comrade would sidestep the question.

"Should we go after him?" Taunauk asked.

Helesys reached out tentatively with her gauntlet, feeling the magic of the seams, like the ebb of a wave as it pulled out to see before growing again. She saw worlds—innumerable worlds. It felt as if each time she peered across the realms that her prowess and her vantage grew.

Here, atop the Godpeak, she saw *everything*. The worlds stretched out, like twinkling glare across an ocean or the uncountable stars in the night sky. There were too many to take in, and so Helesys focused on just a few.

She felt Shawn, the ghostly visage of him riding the currents between worlds, surfing between them. Riding on dreams.

With an aching chest, she turned from him and back to the castle—the dungeon. And within its walls she found another vast sky full of realms. Somewhere within the gargantuan, impossible structure were the abandoned barracks—the realm ruled by Zhug. There they would find the means to delve beneath the sea and claim the Machine of Antrikaumora. Then they would find the Wolf King.

"To task," Helesys said. "We stay the course, to Zhug and then to find the Machine. Shawn will find us, or we will find him after."

Taunauk nodded in solidarity. "Lead the way."

~ ~ ~

<u>From the Author</u>: Shawn will be appearing again alongside Helesys and Taunauk again in the main series. But in the meantime, he'll be off on his own short adventure.

If you want to read about Shawn's encounters across the realms sign up for my Monthly Newsletter at SamuelFlemingBooks.com and you'll get <u>four short stories</u> featuring Shawn. New shorts with the lovable rogue will be coming every two months or so, and delivered right to your Email.

If you like the cover art, you can also get Free Phone and Desktop Backgrounds featuring art from *A Battleaxe and a Metal Arm*!

By signing up, you'll also be the first to hear about publishing news and sales alerts.

Don't like spam? Me neither. You'll get 2-3 Emails at first, all containing the above-mentioned free stuff. After that, expect 1-2 Emails a month.

~ ~ ~

NEXT TIME ON

*A BATTLEAXE AND
A METAL ARM*

Book 13:


*The Abyssal Machine*

Available April 2022

# Spoiler–Free excerpt from *BAMA 13*

Yet there had been echoes of familiarity even then, and now she could think of no one else she'd rather journey with, save for Shawn.

Helesys looked to her comrade, and found him stoic and intently staring at the torches on the wall. He walked over and in one easy motion, ripped the sconce from the wall. Stone scattered across the ground.

They walked the dusty, torch-lit hallway, their footsteps echoing in the silence.

It wasn't long before Helesys had the feeling of being watched. It was heavy and loomed over them—the touch of a powerful mage who did not hide their power.

She smiled and turned toward the scrying eye of the mage. It hung in front of them, some ten feet away, near the ceiling of the hall. Helesys *felt* there was an outline, the vaguest circular shape against the stone, but she couldn't be sure if her eyes were seeing anything or if it was her latent magical sense.

Taunauk too, was staring at the scrying eye as if he could see it though Helesys had no idea how the barbarian was sensing its presence.

"So, you've come back." The giant's gravelly voice rumbled through the hall.

"We need your help," Helesys said.

## To be continued April 2022

# Thank you for Reading

I hope you enjoyed reading this story as much as I enjoyed writing it.

If you did, I would massively appreciate a short review on Amazon or your favorite book website. Reviews are crucial for any author, and a starred review or even just a line or two can make a huge difference.

It's especially true for the start of a series. Thanks and I hope you enjoy the next one!

# Looking for more Engrossing Fantasy?

You might like *Tales from Another World,* an ongoing short story series containing stories about sorcerers, druids, mortals, gods, thieves, and all other manner of Terrans.

The 2nd and 3rd installments are out and they tie into the outside world of *A Battleaxe and a Metal Arm.* So, if you're looking for more engrossing fantasy stories, and if you want to know more about this fantasy universe, read on and see how deep the rabbit hole goes.

# What questions do you have about *A Battleaxe and a Metal Arm*?

If you've read this far, hopefully you'll read a bit further—both in this book and across the series. I'm not sure how most authors write serials and how much of it is flying by the seat of their pants, but that's not how I do things. For all the major questions that might come up in BAMA, I already have answers for 95% of them. Same goes for the major plot points, twists and climaxes. That might sound boring to some, especially some of you other authors who enjoy variations of writing into the dark, but I think having a solid blueprint is paramount to writing a long series.

So, what questions do you have about the story? Here are a few:

1) ~~What is the dungeon?~~ It's a soul trap of overwhelming size and power. But where did it come from? Is it a force of nature or an ill-made weapon, or perhaps something else entirely? In the real world, it looks like a giant cloud with faces writhing just beneath the surface. Helesys speculates that the

reason no one remembers it is because it's so horrific their minds blot it out!

2) ~~Who was Helesys before she got trapped~~? We've learned that Helesys was both a soldier and was the oldest daughter of the elven Great House Byyra.

3) ~~Who was Taunauk before he got trapped~~? There was an omen of a blight in the Endroggen heaven, Accaelum. Taunauk is an Endroggen barbarian who was raised as a warrior and a vessel. His purpose was to one day free the trapped Endroggen souls from the Dungeon.

4) How well did they know each other beforehand?

5) How did Helesys get her metal arm? Likely through injury, amputation, and replacement. She was likely fighting in the Eternal War, the war of the Elves against the Shadowkind.

6) ~~Who is Shawn~~? He is a wisp from the plane of dreams. One who walks through the dreams of elves and humans, while being neither. He has lived as both a god and a mortal.

7) Why does Shawn feel so familiar to Helesys and Taunauk? The group speculates that they were traveling together for unknown reasons. Shawn worries that they were tracking him. This could explain why Helesys and Taunauk are always reborn together, while Shawn was usually alone.

7) Who is the Wolf King and what sinister plans does he have for our heroes? How did he come to rule over the Dungeon? How does the Gatekeeper factor into all this?

8) Who is the mysterious voice encountered on the white sandy shores of Meridian? Why do they seek the death of the Wolf-King? …And why did they choose the heroes?

Did I miss any questions? Probably. Connect with me and other *BAMA* fans on social media and compare questions!

I've got plans. I've got answers. And I've got them on a drip-feed. Keep reading and expect to find out a little more to the mysteries with each installment. Hopefully, you're as excited about this series as I am.

# Connect with the Author

If you want to stay up to date on the latest about Samuel's publishing news and blog, check out his website and consider signing up for his monthly newsletter.

www.SamuelFlemingBooks.com

Samuel can also be found on Reddit, Goodreads and Facebook.

Samuel Fleming is a Science Fiction and Fantasy author.

He grew up in Maryland, spending most of his time swimming and writing. Swimming gave him a lot of time to daydream, so the two hobbies complemented each other well. Idle day dreams turned into stories, some of which stuck with him for years. These days he swims a little less and writes a lot more.

He loves a good story no matter the medium: Books, TV, video games, comics, tabletop RPG's, or podcasts—most of which he attempts to share with his wife and three kids, and occasionally on his blog.